If this document should survive

Robin Wyatt Dunn

By Robin Wyatt Dunn

POETRY
Poems from the War
Science Fiction: a poem!
Sunsborne
Wine Country
What Black Delirious Daylight Sets You Forward in the Boat
Remarriages
Debudaderrah
Black Heart Uprising
Some Dredged Deep
Death Songs

NOVELS
Los Angeles, or American Pharaohs
My Name is Dee
Fighting Down into the Kingdom of Dreams
Line to Night Island
A Map of Kex's Face
Julia, Skydaughter
Conquistador of the Night Lands
White Man Book
Colonel Stierlitz
Black Dove
City, Psychonaut
2DEE
Now the last light
This isn't one of the stories I remember
The Black King of Kalfour
Sitting on the Floor
City, Winter

By Robin Wyatt Dunn

NON-FICTION
Refugees from America

SHORT STORIES
Dark is a Color of the Day

PLAYS
Last Freedom

FILMS
A Wilderness in Your Heart
Party Games
American Messenger

JOHN OTT
TUCSON, ARIZONA
2022

ISBN - 978-1-940830-36-0
LOC - 2022933950

Cover art by Barbara Sobczyńska

Note: the scorpion separator is based
upon the etching of Luigi Conconi's
monotype frontispiece, 1884.

for Beatrice

If this document should survive—and I mean for it to—let it be both revelator and curse for whoever discovers it. Let these memories be preserved out of my own ornery insistence on the matter, and let that the act be a weapon—but not yours.

These are the things I comfort myself with when I consider my current circumstances—to say that they are "reduced," would be generous. But as in all such things ...

But I am delaying.

I work at the office and there is a woman there with great scorpions in her hair. They are dead, you understand, we are in the desert. But sometimes they look like they might be alive, when she is curled over her desk, watching the numbers flick over the screen, and I reach into my pants to ...

But what was it I was trying to say. Oh yes, welcome to hell. The word means cavern and so my surmise is that these reaches extend quite a further way down. I must serve as a kind of syphilitic Dante, in this realm that is not a realm—or anyway not a supernatural one.

It is Arizona.

We don't know what the name means: it could be "oaks," or "stream." Some ordinary name. I prefer to think of it as The Zone. Like Interzone, but not as gay. Neither happy nor homosexual, you understand. We diddle few boys here, though I am sure the practice has not been eradicated. But the other side: everything else that lived in that more famous Zone lives here in abundance, as my Scorpion Woman can attest.

I shall be a Tall Dark and Mysterious Man who Arrived from No Particular Place with Various Mental Illnesses—the height of Romance— and she shall be a syrupy faun dredged up out of the lake (though none such exists in this state)—a kind of negative Lady of the Lake,

Lady Without a Lake, but with Many Scorpions in her hair, and the same Demon Affliction as her more watery sister, tempted by the forces of the deep.

There are so many, and from all directions. It is quite impossible to describe. Why then, do I attempt it? Because to return to the office is worse. In these moments I need not contemplate the Screen and its Many Dastardly Deeds, and more importantly, cogitate on what kind of thing it is making me become.

Here, with you, I can feel almost human. Like a brother, or a son. One who committed crimes and was cast out and now exists in relation to you as a kind of uncomfortable wart, that you are not quite ready to remove. Love, in other words. This is something that we share.

The town is, I am tempted to say, nondescript, but that is only because its mode and color is so deeply familiar to me that I find it terrifying.

Miles of gas stations. Strip malls of all description. Fast food joints and above it all the mountains, leering like a corpse from a budget horror flick, the last bastion of a civilization blasted into dust, and leaving us here, a remnant ...

Not The Remnant, you understand, as I don't go in for that Bible Shit, though there are plenty here that do, but a remnant nevertheless, one uncomfortable with its inheritance.

Though inheritance is not the right word. Curse? No. Legacy? Also not quite right. Found object is closer. Though it is we who are the foundlings. And found by whom?

I dare not ask ... but I do dare ... but not yet.

My favorite stories have always had a kind of dark gloom cast over them, and now I am almost afraid that this one contains too much light—because that is all Arizona has, in the end, miles and miles of light. Even at midnight it seems to stream in from all directions.

Perhaps I shall have to exaggerate a bit but that

feels wrong somehow—no matter that it is the mainstay of narrative ever since the first time a man caught a fish. Some cousin to the verb then—like a man simplifies a woman's body in his mind, reducing her to tits, waist, and ass, let this too be such a simplification, of The Dark Hand who hovers over us all, to terrify the children and make them loyal and obedient citizens of this prison.

The monster inside—inside the earth and sky but more importantly inside the head. When it reveals its face. Or when it covers it up. When the Devil demands his due obeisances from all his willing slaves ...

Romantic again, I know. I am a Romantic man—born at the wrong time. Or at the right time in the wrong body ... but I am delaying again. You see how difficult it is for me.

The center of our existence: the office. Though already I feel that I am lying. Behind each door in Kafka's castle is yet a greater one, with yet more terrifying a visage.

But one door at a time, old friend. Let us describe this one first.

I am not yet ready to go into it. Let us stand outside for a minute and admire the landscape. The banking tower, standing like Atlas holding up the sky of phony money, blinking his red light. And the arroyo, overgrown with weeds and filled with aluminum cans and plastic bags and an abandoned shopping cart that stands like an obscure shrine, half buried in the duff.

The arroyo cuts back and forth across the corporate parking lot and then heads down to the street, set in with rocks and covered in trees—beautiful. The best spot around for a mile. The cats love it and come here to hunt. We get hawks too, chasing the pigeons. Where the arroyo crosses the parking lot and heads into the street it goes into concrete tubes, and the final one is marked with a Stephen King warning painted above it:

"It's cool down here." Which is both literally

true, a good place to hide in the heat of summer when it is 110 degrees here, and other things we had best not name, not yet ...

But the orange cat knows, when I asked him. The arroyo is his domain, whenever he is away from wherever it is that he is fed. He knows that the tube leads to deeper regions.

I am almost ready to go inside. I have my RFID badge which I refuse to wear around my neck like a dog collar; I shove it in my pocket instead and whip it out at the scanning boxes. I have my corporate coffee mug, almost the size of my head, emblazoned in our green corporate logo. Sealed with two layers of aluminum, so that my neurological poisoning can occur at a pleasurable temperature.

I go into the office, where we are come to greet the day in silence, as guardians before the deep:

Each inside of our cube. Each one of us marked by God, for sacrifice.

I should be getting ready for bed but your ears (eyes?)—brain?—you have drawn me back again. Thank you for that. It is good to know I have some place to go.

The wind is rising over the desert, and the cold setting in. Saturn approaches Jupiter here in this apocalyptic year, revelation of revelations ... no Bible stuff! Absolutely not. Science! Jesus! And other anomalies ...

I am living in an apartment near the office, here in Arizona. Please allow me to describe it. It has the usual amenities: parking, pool, laundry. Cops who show up. Rent-a-cops who show up. Some of the area billboards say THANK A COP. Other cars bear bumper stickers which read: THANK A COP. None of them have bothered me yet. As some of my friends have reminded me from time to time, I am the right color.

The right color for what? Well, to be left alone, such as we are. Alone with our own devices!

Our new and frightening devices ... that are no longer really ours ...

But it is a good place to live. Again because we are left alone, for the most part. Unlike in England, I do not need to write any council and inform them I have arrived. That a new and warm taxpaying body is in the vicinity. Of course Arizona easily divests me of its due, through payroll taxes, but the distinction is important. We can pretend.

The moon is bright above. I have fed myself. This device on which I write, manufactured in China, sends its radiations through my body, looking for answers and loyalties. It seeks to install a plug in me, like the Baron Vladimir Harkonnen on Geidi Prime: a heart plug which can be removed at the first sign of his displeasure ...

We have trees, and cats. Dogs on leashes. Even a small dog park. They have installed solar panels above the parking lots, providing shade. Huge red boxes (manufactured in Canada! They declare) purport to be battery packs of some sort for the solar. And perhaps have other functions, just like my Chinese book ...

There are things I must say but please allow me to sidle up to them, sidelong, gentle. It is only that I am afraid, not only of myself, but for you. Add to that the fact that I have no answers whatsoever, only questions.

The questions are enough. They are dangerous now that governments have become nervous.

What a thing a question is! How divine! How simple. Something every child—no matter how brain damaged through no fault of its own—still conjures. The leading up to the edge and looking down ... out over the city ... out over the land. What a place we have come to.

Tell me, won't you, what the most important thing is. Is it sex? I am almost celibate—no story there. Children? Nothing there either. God? This would be tedious. Science? No, no. The truth? I've grown fond of it, of course, but no.

Something else. What is it? The story itself—trying to find it. It is not true, impossible that it should be. Nor is it a lie. It is a story.

The scorpion girl. She is quite beautiful. A young mother. She has a son who I have never seen. Women haunt me in their dreams. My dreams?

Well. The story then. The kind of knowledge it dictates. Not truth, nor science. This weapon that the story is. Yes, it's a war story. I see that now. I am sorry that it should be that but remember:

Oh remember dear heart.

The chief weapon in this war is forgetfulness.

1.

The naked mask of pleasure is a mask of hate, or so for the managers, of which I am one, reluctantly. We are trying to escape, like Moses. The Phoenicians to whom we are indebted for the chronicles of Byblos—and their religion/ weapon of blasting the world into ash so that they can rule the remains—includes within it like the Wachovskis' Matrix included the Neo-function, this longing to get out.

Every time I try to get out, they pull me back in! We should interrogate Pacino and his friends—no question—but that joy will have to be saved for another day.

The burning questions of the day. My own pitiful contributions to this litany of moans and regrets. Beseeching and quarrelling and arguing with God, like a good Jew. Who are we and why did we come here?

Were we a mining expedition as my friend Mike Ferreira avers? Are we alien colonists as the Slavic Vedas claim? Are we genetic experiments from monkeys, a la Elijah Mohammed? So many fun possibilities, all of them somehow depressing.

In the meantime the situation is the same: tightening manacles. Reduced diet. Increased exercises (or the denial of it entirely). More propaganda. Petty shame-exercises. New kinds of torture—the same as the old kind, in a new package.

The name of the word inside your belly, indigestible, you golem. Raised from Earth as Frankenstein's man-shape to puzzle out the shape of the world.

I should salute you but I am too tired. Here, accept this handshake, now forbidden. Feel my hand and know that I am a man.

2.

Consider Bruce Springsteen's magnum opus "State Trooper" as a Phoenician plot arc—quasi Mad-Max tall dark handsome stranger bound on an illegal mission across the blasted plain to deliver to his beloved some unspoken horror—

The name of the ruler. The arc of the galaxy. The shape of the exit. The bonds of flesh tying us to this plane, and beyond it.

The Phoenicians who would destroy and rebuild the state. Desiring to be both sides: monarch and revolutionary.

The radio relay towers will lead us to our baby, but is it Anti-Christ or human child?

Please don't stop me on my mission into the dark heart of the continent ...

I am working for the Mormons. They too have a Phoenician-style religion, both on the face of it and underneath, of being this Remnant— survivors of Apocalypse. Only they to carry the True Word (and all its preferences and pre- rogatives and privileges) into the future, et cet- era et cetera.

They have gotten lazy but are still good slavers: they know enough to love those who labor for them, and desire that these workers should be made hardier and more efficient. They don't know how to achieve this but do desire it.

In this effort I am their overseer now, in the call center where I monitor the calls and speak to the agents and try to get them to be better. More like a machine. Communicate better with the machine and so rise, Pharaoh, from the sleepy death's-head of your tomb, and blaze over the desert ...

It's not so bad! The overseer enjoys certain privileges. More piss breaks. A few extra burritos per month. A special colored badge. The right to participate in certain "appreciation exercises" where we get special shame from the higher-ups, as reminders that we subscribe to their ethos of some inaccessible truth—or accessible only to initiates—hovering just out of sight.

Good workers, in other words. Though we are unable, as the gangs who labored on the pyramids, to inscribe our sigil onto our stone. Nor even, as Warren Robinett in his Adventure to plant an Easter Egg demarcating our identity for future explorers ...

We are like traffic conductors standing inside the blaze of light of the Internet ... just narrowly avoiding being hit by the semis ...

Or perhaps we are the truck drivers, bent on our mission, miles to go before we sleep.

How many is it brother? I am sleeping on my feet.

3.

There's nothing more I can say; I should stop now. Or rather, if I continue I fear I shall never shut up. All of my confessions, theories, hopes, dreams, etc. The whole obscene carnival of Robin's hamster wheel brain shall be opened for you, my beloved, no matter my fear or heartache, I shall keep babbling into the chill of the night air for you:

There are two cop cars outside the supermarket, flashing their lights. Inside the sliding doors, a huge sign commands: WEAR A MASK. I walk by it barefaced, and the cop tips his hat to me, and I go in and buy my milk and tea.

Inside my mind I thought: "I am a child of God."

What kind of absurdity? Both them and me. The best carnival ride you ever saw: totally realistic. Totally depraved. A trip over the edge.

I always wanted to go there, you see. I always wanted to spill right over the edge. Finally I got there. I wish I had known how good it would be so I could have done it sooner.

Lose your mind as soon as possible, children. It's better on the other side.

4.

I am marooned among you; the shipwreck slow and full of noise. Occasional sirens. Mutters and groans. Lights in the sky. Saturn approaches Jupiter, father and son, reunited in the afterlife:

The loan foreclosed. The land sold. We can no longer buy the farm: it has been damned.

The electric vessel of my arms waits for the signal; Dr. Frankenstein and his magic switch; some terrible Jew and his sigil; I am flesh; I wake. These are the musics of the sky: helicopter and drone and bomber, slow and quiet against the grey.

All of the cats are silent. My boss wears a mask and hands me sparkling cider (non-alcoholic; she is a Mormon) in a fluted plastic glass sans ice (as Robert Ashley says), I put it on my desk for the celebration tomorrow:

We will be celebrated for staring at the screen. For recording our neighbors. I am a member of a reluctant and unknowing Stasi, Alexas and Siris made of flesh.

We labor in the mines of phone land for you, my brothers. We are pleased to do it as it forecloses worse disasters, of which there are so many ...

A crisis of the imagination. What can I imagine? What could possibly be imagined?

Not love. Or love, but the horrendous variety of cartoon anvil, tearing open my skull:

Is that what love is?

The sky shadows us and watches for our signals too: are we ready? Willing?

Do we know the consequences of this decision?

Of course we can still say it is comedy; deck chairs on Titanic, love in the ruins; hairstyles never finer, women spending extra time on their legs and hips but then covering their face...

The new religion of some Anti-God waking slow from out the ground, a kind of boring Nick-at-Nite version, with cheap mall white beard.

What do you want for Christmas son?

"I want a puppy!"

And you shall get it boy, all the puppies we can deliver, the Dogs of the Night, roaring your holy name!

"Mommy!"

They shall be cloaked in fineries beyond description and you their master boy but they want to hunt! Can you make the dogs hunt boy?

5.

Nothing is visible—not even you. We're buried under the earth, dried up gnomes stuck to the walls, still wondering how far it is we can go.

I can go downstairs to the laundry room, through the terrible masquerade, which is still recognizably human. A stolen garbage can, a man filling the barbecue with flames. The sky is slate and the stars are reluctant to reveal to us how far we've come; how much they know.

It doesn't matter—they know enough, and so do you—and we are stuck to the ribbon being pulled slow through the projector.

See, here are my arms, displayed against my face. Here my body a statue against the evening, like the water silo stands beneath the times coming, and soon gone:

Years of plenty, and of want. All that we want here is silence, hard to come by. The open road. The nectar of the gods. Children's laughter. The names of friends dead. The armature of the heavens, obsene in its beauty, reminds us of the necessary tasks before us: all of heaven's games, nurtured and sad and ornery, fauns and fairies ecstatic and determined:

To get their due.

No one shall get theirs here. It is not in the cards.

I have been playing a video game: my little men collect berries and fruit. The buildings rise, tenements, for their orchards and fields. For their electronic eyes.

They are robots, set against the day. Their distant hope, so far away that they are unable to describe it, is the dream, like Martin Luther King's, set out against the color of the sky, black and indignant in rage, the magus descending to the dais for his poem:

Escape.

The last dollar hidden away inside our pants
and jealously guarded. The hole card. And the
whole card. A map of a world.

A river running beneath, hideously beautiful,
lonely. Alph who turns his eye to laugh at our
battered frame and visage.

Our translator from this world into the next:

6.

Soon I'll be a savage, able to kill without re-
morse—or at least without the appearance of
it. Soon all morals will be taken away except
whatever compass I bear inside, pointing …
where?

My lodestone spins and so do I, anchorless, the
horizon a sheet of lightning—

Tell me the meaning: that is, what you can
agree on.

Are we God's chosen? Chosen to do what?
The best men to send into the mine … and then
men like me, to count the carts that come out.

Good job, Johnson, eight today. Stevenson,
only five? Step it up there.

Me with my pencil, clipboard and pocket pro-
tector, my white linen and my black ink both
shining:

I shall write the narrative of thee, who steps

down into the earth-beast to hear her voices and protect us against the watchful eyes of gods unfriendly to this zone ... to burn the incense of the smoke rock and so disguise the electric lines inside our nerves ...

A problem with the nerves. A problem with the brain. A probe sent in to find just what the obstruction is:

We've got a man here Johnny. He won't come out.

What does he want Frederic?

He wants to know what it means, Johnny. Says he's got questions.

Blow him up, Freddy. We don't need any of that. I'll send down the dynamite.

He shall say: Dynamite me father for I have sinned. It has been years since my last confession—I never really did it. I'm a Protestant. An atheist. A lunatic. A writer, father. I did bad things.

That's all right, son. God forgives you. But the mining company says you've got another six months on your contract.

7.

There are things that need to be said—although really, they already have been. I suppose I'm saying they need to be said again. But that's not right either. It isn't enough—not yet—the complaints and essays and objections and protests and signs and plagues. Not of any invisible pathogen—or anyway, nothing external. The plague within is not yet enough: we have to do more.

We really have to set you to unease. Dis-ease. Make you see the bite of food on the end of every fork, the ultimate and unrealized goal of Naked Lunch. Perhaps the heroin addicts were right: it is the universe next door which has the meanings that we need, if we are to live.

The door into heaven, that is also the door into this world. Who do you believe? Do you even believe yourself? Is that the hardest part?

To believe in your own eyes.

Your ears. The immediate exculpatory reality

of it. That is: you are vindicated if you let your eyes and ears work. And blame can be turned to where it better lies.

What does it take to see and hear? Its own immensity: the tangent and fervor of the apparati and their indignities: not as Joyce would have it the inexorable modality ...

No. Eyes and ears are neither inexorable nor a mode. They are so easily superseded. That is why we are in the problem we are in. If we were all Stephen Daedalus, ready to strap our boy into the waxen wings ...

But we are not.

These eyes and ears are machines glued into our bodies to tell us what is real.

Real enough for government work, motherfucker. And if you govern with me, by my side, inside the leash of time, I will love you. I'll kill for you. But that understanding necessitates its cousins of the leash of the senses themselves: to know that they know more than you. They have been here before. You are a visitor. You are the new boss.

You have been flown in, brother. Welcome back. I am your sergeant and my duty is to inform you that your body is a weapon, filled with a black galaxy of knowledge, still accessible and ready for use, by you, private. We are at war.

These are your eyes, set inside of your head. One or two or three, it does not matter. They will tell you what is up and above and below and beside you. Pay attention to what it is they might teach you.

Here are your ears, wide and ugly on the sides of your barren head. What a lovely head! I'll bash it in! I promise.

With these ears you can divine the smallest movements. In this galaxy and those neighboring. Your body and others'. Ears can penetrate this darkness of the world even better than the eye. They can see anything—at great distance. Where are we?

8.

The girl with scorpions in her hair no longer loves me; so now I have another love, in the way of office politics, where no one can say what they mean, and we are all constrained by the all consuming love of money, or hatred of money, but never indifference to money, whose name divines her origin in Minerva, the ultimate fucking housewife.

Hausfrau from hell, come calling down, demanding:

Pleading:

Insisting:

To balance that fucking checkbook.

To balance the checkbook of love, not even the gods are sufficient force. Its imaginary plane—outside of and interpenetrating ours— keeps track of every little movement of the eye. Every second's posture. An accounting method writ into the genes and into the soul, where nothing is forgotten, and everything is recorded.

Hell, in other words.

I grow horns on my head. I am sharpening my farming tool, barbed and wicked, with which to probe the earth:

Hell is only a cave, lit by fluorescent lights, and armed with cameras and RFIDs, the stool pigeons of history come down to roost and forget about their crimes ...

Who can you decide to love? Is it a decision? What bond insists upon it? Whose entry point—in which direction—and for whose history, divine and manmade, do I block the mind to receive the gift, of one glance:

Lighting curls slow over her thought, and in mine. Like a good ranger, burnt hot by the divine fire, napalm and mustard gas, I leak my fluids blood and mucus from the open nuclear sores to return—joyously acclaimed—to deliver my indifferent report:

Well, here it comes again. I got nothing else to say. No one else could move me now. One of you try.

9.

Writing is a kind of grave-robbing: robbing from your future self to pay your past. I don't know what that means, but I wrote it. What does this say about writing?

This question I have a better handle on: writing is the best expression of a temporary overlap. Self and other. No one ever writes for themselves. They write as part of this transition and negotiation between the self and everyone else.

About the past and future I have no idea: you know better than me. The present is all that concerns me. This terrible gift.

I have been blessed by god with this stubbornness I keep using—if stubbornness were a kind of eye. What good is it? What good is it to know the present?

This question is related to the hippy cliché: "live in the moment." I inquire after this present moment but the act of inquiry must take me out of that present moment and then elsewhere. It is a tension. We have to go places and the stubborn man is often in a position to advise on where might be most useful ...

I'm sorry. You see that I am distraught. All of this is a mediation of pain. Where did it come from and how can I use it, combat it, harness it, overcome it. Overcoming seems too far away for me; I have to settle for some compromise. A battle I can win at minimal cost—or perhaps even better, a battle I can lose and gain from later.

The ingenious amateur historian Dan Carlin of "Hardcore History" claims that it took millennia of warfare to produce an army that could "take a hit" without crumbling—one large and well-armed enough to lose a substantial portion of its men but remain in fighting spirit ... (And that would be World War One Germany...)

But the best writers were here before the best general. We know the value of losing.

Really, I have been winning; after a long time.

This is part of my anxiety—am I forcing you to be a shrink?—no, no, anything but that. Do not shrink me. It isn't that I propose to use myself as a stand-in for your experience, or that I desire for you to explain to me what it means that I am where I am and feel how I feel. I trust merely that it might have some use. That these times might be used to squeeze out some juice which can be salvaged ...

What does it mean to write. To salvage these experiences. It is like a random photographer, drop-shipped on some planet and some culture he has no knowledge about, invited to use his camera.

I have finished my work. The water is trickling in the bathroom. The moon is bright and the stars are dim here in the city; the people are quiet. I long to know what I can still do: what I am capable of.

How did I create so many enemies? I never intended to. I loved too much, perhaps. Or was too stubborn, or both.

10.

Now and we'll escape. Now and the door will open … Aladdin and Merlin and my Fairy Godmother wielding a mighty mace, standing at the door …

All doors out lead in; eternal waking; the most woke of the woke; out of the world.

Out of this world lies the world: yet again. Death hardly even a detail. But in the meantime:

I find myself occupied with the question of who I can trust.

The most paranoid, cut off, and unapproachable man, woman, cat and child suddenly the best possible companion …

The warlike tribe is the most amenable to honorable dealings, since they are willing to enforce whatever contracts they enter into as a group. The peaceloving ones will roll over at the first sign of conflict …

Roll over and play dead, motherfucker.

But even a dog has his limits: those things he is not willing to do. And the etymology of war suggests it is less about mounting warriors in battlefields and more about navigating schizophrenia of various kinds: nightmare landscapes devoid of people. The ultimate interior lockdown. War means confusion.

Dance with me, though it be death, and be rewarded, with the exquisite sense that it was worth it, and that you paid the highest possible price.

11.

Escape at root means "get out of your cape"—
to shuck out of your dress and slip away. A
kind of nakedness—the thrill of return.

Return to what? In escaping, what are we re-
turning to? The Garden of Eden? Eden means
some combination of "pleasurable, well-wa-
tered plain"—somehow I don't think that's
where we're going. Some Ur before Ur ... a root
of roots. We'll be escaping not only our cape
but our head as well ...

And linking up with that ur-matter—the mi-
asmus and shield spirit who encompasses this
Earth, of which we are a part ...

A kind of absurd Voltron. *E Pluribus Unum* and
all that. But One What?

12.

We're almost at the end of it—lies doing what lies do. You forget about them, sometimes. Sometimes they make you angry. Sometimes they turn into yet greater lies. The episode—not entirely satisfying, but somehow worthwhile—coming to its stubborn close.

The denouement—a word that means untying—coming slow and solemn against our back.

If I untie you, will you run? Will you kiss me? In your terrible freedom to which I am bonded, will I be graced with your solitude as well? And what do you have for me, in your face? A secret door, clutched and trembling thrust against the night.

It's slow, the waking up. The light not quite right. The clouds uncertain. The people can't quite remember who they are.

And they're being told. Ever more forcefully ...

A man, man.

These little stubborn battles. The signs at the supermarket. The masks hanging from rear view mirrors: empty scrotums.

We're patient like men are, watching the enemy come close.

13.

The writer is not god but seeks to become like him, believing god to be permanent—a feature of the landscape not subject to erosion.

If this document should survive five minutes. If it should live that long: be known that long. From one minute to the next. This already is some indicator of its worth—if only for this hour.

This hour's worth—however unquantifiable—stretches the imagination to include those parts of ourselves most interesting to writers: the landscape and spirit inside.

In longing for the survivability of the document, we ultimately argue for some imperishability of the soul. The writer is asking: please let me be counted.

Please notice me, divines, the writer says—I have something that I want to say.

14.

What is it that women want? The Biblical position—the missionary position?

—but I can't. What, am I going to give you aphorisms?

Aphorism at root means "mark off, divide, bound." Shall I be Moses and give you law? Lol

Lawl too has lost its sense of "lots of laughs" and become more lulz, or lull: a sweeping smear, a swear word.

A form of fuck.

Women desire of course that grisly cup so famous in Revelations but the problem is that we appear so eager to give it to them. Desire is the stars but we are the something else.

Bounded and bearded and bedroom-eyed—absurd but no less honorable for our famed butt-of-all-jokes.

I swore to finish what I started, but what I've started now is too many things ... one thing at a time, Robin.

Moses only means son. Drawn out from the water to grow into a man. Should we drown him now? This patriarch, and his absurd journey to nowhere at all, is no less honorable for all that.

And it is woman remember, who bears the shield: for both the Greeks and the Romans. She wields it up and over her man, on every coin we can find.

Man means "hand." And woman means "clit hand." All men are born also with one, but then sealed up in the womb, stitched from scrotum to anus to seal us up and mark us for duty, to convince this creature that she had better wait.

Wait, child, for the water:

15.

It's said that once a family produces a writer, that family is destroyed. My aunt once told me, half-jokingly, when I repeated this to her: "We'll kill you before that happens."

Family, all familiar things, destroyed by writers, in our lust or desire, helpless headlong rush into the unexplored regions of the soul.

I, no longer familiar, hail you from the country and kingdom of my own, unspeakable, untranslatable, already dead, not yet born, infringing by definition on all you know.

We're coming in baby. Tell me that you could hail us on arrival in words of your own: that you will recognize this unrecognizable call when it comes, to lay down your weapons and laugh, at this colossal joke:

Once a family produces a writer. Strange egg, imperfectly incubated, perfectly and logically leashed to a chain of being, but deriding that logic on its fruition:

Apology or confession? J'accuse? Well. This is only a book: most useful of all things, and most beloved. Like loving god, murderous fakir laughing with your heart in his mouth.

16.

Love at root is the same word as leave: to grant permission.

Not everything is permitted; and though I should fear you you give me strength, under the board, under the terrible actors' board, raging over our heads. Come with me, mechanical, and trade with me the light above for the light below, our secret affair of the deeds never spoken, hinted at above:

The smudges and shimmers in your waist. Whatever is recorded, set to the body, turned into the canon, sacreded and secreted away for the voyage—

Well, it is a Romantic fable. Better perhaps to see this as already erased—anxiety or no, worth or no, meaning or meaningless—just another detail in the swath of destruction.

The Scorpion Woman is trembling and so am I; for I am infected by the midnight ray—Cthulu's arm—come all so close to us now courtesy of our government.

So tell me anything you can remember. Tell it to me soft and low so that they will not hear, or if they hear they will not listen, and if they listen they will not record, or if recorded, it will be filed away in some forgotten catacomb and not discovered until we are long dead, and our civilization turned all to dust, like your face ...

I will love you still; but know, that it served a purpose, over and above these signs and trage-dies and my pleas over the carriage of my feet and voice—so naïve, and adolescent—

Still, while I am both things, to my shame, I come before you in honor to request that the transmission be preserved. Not for knowledge only—not for ego only—not only lust calls me to plead—the honor is some other kind.

The kind a king might have when he is dying, and desires that the story shake some founda-tion in some kingdom long after he is ash.

The kind a girl has holding a flower, beholding the entire world.

About the author

Robin Wyatt Dunn was born in Wyoming in 1979. You can read more of his work at www.robindunn.com.